Just Another Day In Hell

LIANA BROOKS

OTHER WORKS

ALL I WANT FOR CHRISTMAS

All I Want For Christmas Is A Reaper
All I Want For Christmas Is A Werewolf

FLEET OF MALIK

Bodies In Motion
Change of Momentum

HEROES AND VILLAINS

Even Villains Fall In Love
Even Villains Go To The Movies
Even Villains Have Interns
Even Villains Play The Hero (books 1 – 3 omnibus)
The Polar Terror

TIME AND SHADOWS

The Day Before
Convergence Point
Decoherence

SHORTER WORKS

Fey Lights
Prime Sensations
Darkness and Good

Find other works by the author at
www.lianabrooks.com

Just Another Day In Hell

INKLET #86

LIANA BROOKS

Inkprint PRESS

www.inkprintpress.com

Print ISBN: 978-1-922434-26-5
eBook ISBN: 9798201588397

www.inkprintpress.com

National Library of Australia Cataloguing-in-Publication Data
Brooks, Liana 1982 –
Just Another Day In Hell
46 p.
ISBN: 978-1-922434-26-5
Inkprint Press, Canberra, Australia
1. Fiction—Fantasy—Contemporary 2. Fiction—
Fantasy—Paranormal 3. Fiction—Occult & Supernatural

First Print Edition: July 2022
Cover photo © daria_lukoiko via Deposit Photos
Cover design © Inkprint Press
Interior art © Amy Laurens

WELCOME TO
HELL
ENJOY YOUR JOURNEY

JUST ANOTHER DAY
IN HELL

Lava gurgled over opened fissures in the walls as, in the distance, the voices of the damned screamed for mercy. The air didn't smell of sulfur or burning tires, no matter what anyone said in their religious soliloquies; it smelled of damp earth with a touch of rotten potato, and lingering mold from the humid season in Florida.

And mothballs.

Not because Hell smells of mothballs naturally, but some young buck had had the bright idea to introduce mothballs to Hell and now the smell stuck like a bad memory.

Grantupoemoeunanii, Keeper of Memories and Mortal Forms, trundled through their small office at the south-west corner of the Eternal Infernal Hall. That was the official name printed on all the pamphlets sent out by head office, though the hall was neither eternal or altogether infernal. Not unless one thought lava oozing across the broken, pock-marked floor with the occasional jazz rift breaking the boundaries of Heaven infernal.

There were donuts in the break room—the good kind—and better wages and vacation plans than even Sweden had. Really, at the end of the day, caring for the damned souls throwing tantrums rather than going to Heaven was just another heavenly job. Albeit a heavenly job that shopped at the Halloween Outlet store.

With a breathy sigh that summoned memories of bitter autumn winds and grave dirt, Grantupoemoeunanii dropped into their IKAE chair (like IKEA but actually well-made and easy to put together). Today was going to be like the last two million, five hundred fifty-five days that had gone on before. There would be paperwork, a small memo, perhaps a slice of birthday cake, and then Grantupoemoeunanii would trundle home to the bungalow they shared with Erowbbaia, Keeper of Lost Socks and Answerer of Prayers To Saint Anthony (when they involved lost socks), overlooking Elysium, the paradise for humans who died while the Greeks ruled the world.

The both of them lived on the hellish side by choice. The coffee was better and so was the beat poetry.

That was the only noticeable difference between Heaven and Hell. Many a damned soul sat weeping bitterly at the gates of the Heavens, cursing in their native tongues and railing against the creator of the universe when all they had to do was stop blubbering and actually walk on through the door to Heaven.

It wasn't as if it was ever locked.

The newer Heavens didn't even put up proper doors, just wide open fields and a little sign that read "Welcome to Heaven" in a friendly font.

Grantupoemoeunanii shook their head and sipped an exquisite dark roast while looking over the day's docket. Looked like Keighbii was going up to tempt a politician again. That had to be a boring job. Poor demon.

And Wiebbitma was going to tempt a priest, didn't say which denomination but there was a note about the requisitioned body needing a smartphone with PokemonGo installed, so it was probably a young one.

Wouldn't do much good though, all it took to get into heaven wa—

A gust of wind that smelled of bus stations, deli meat and Chicago pizza made Grantupoemoeunanii look up at the Eternal Infernal Hall and then at the clock. Work didn't start for another ten minutes. Who could possibly be returning on such short notice?

So untidy. So inconsiderate!

The heat of Hell blistered a rock, popping it so sulfurous steam and molten rock spewed across the hall.

The incoming demon sidestepped this with a little nose wrinkle on their face.

Grantupoemoeunanii frowned and tried to place the body. It was feminine in a uniquely human way, curvy with a bright pink shirt and faded blue jeans with artistic rips in it. Brown hair was tied up in a messy bun with a shimmering butterfly pin.

Really, it looked like millions of other human bodies, except this demon was walking with a noticeable limp as it approached Grantupoemoeunanii's office.

The incoming demon waved as they approached. "Hi."

"Good morning. I am Grantupoemoeunanii, Keeper of Memories and Mortal Forms, are you picking up or dropping off?" They looked at the human body with distaste. There was no obvious external damage, but humans were so terribly frail. "If you've injured this body there will be fines, naturally. The paperwork does say so."

"Ah."

The demon looked uneasy, as far as Grantupoemoeunanii was capable of reading human facial expressions.

Grantupoemoeunanii smiled, stretching a face with the taste and texture of a red gummy bear into a wide grin. "First time out? It's unnerving out there, isn't it? Dealing with creatures who only understand linear time and can't foresee the obvious consequence of their own actions. Quite bewildering. Just tell me what you did to the body."

"Ah, well, that's the thing." The demon perched their borrowed human elbows on the counter. "The body came to me this way. Quite broken. Joints are a mess. The brain on this one—whooo!—not good. It's wobbly. Sometimes the legs give out. It aches all the time. Constant, constant pain. I was hoping I could just, you know, pick up a new one."

Grantupoemoeunanii raised their eyebrows. "A new one?"

"Yeah, I mean, the design isn't bad." The demon gestured to their human form. "The hair color is a bit bland. The height is not great. Um, admittedly I'm very average looking, but I can live with that. It's the pain that I can't handle."

"It's a lovely body," Grantupoemoeunanii said, patting the demon's human form. "I mean, not quite as lovely as your natural form, but for a human shape it's perfectly lovely. Now, let's see…" They pulled out a pair of gold-rimmed spectacles and a computer for the look of the thing. "…How long have you had this form?"

"Twenty-three years on Saturday."

"Mortal or infernal years?"

"Mortal?"

A whole twelve minutes in infernal time.

Grantupoemoeunanii sighed again and somewhere a coffin cracked. "Really, that's hardly any time at all. Can I do a scan?"

"Sure?" The young demon sounded confused, maybe even agitated.

Grantupoemoeunanii patted their hand again, leaving cherry-flavored residue behind. "Done in a jiff. It won't hurt." The little machine was hardly more than a heavenly essence scanner re-jigged to check for damage to human bodies returned for infernal processing and refurbishing, but it looked impressive in the big silver box, rows of flashing red lights, and speaker that screamed BEEP! loud enough to be heard three Heavens over.

A push. A fluttering of lights. A beep that shook the foundations of Hell.

And then a little tickertape produced a readout.

"Oh, dear," Grantupoemoeunanii said, breathing out thorns of winter and the scent of ground pepper. "Bless my infernal soul."

"Is there a problem?" The little demon stood on tiptoe, trying to peek at the readout.

"Extreme damage to the joints. Early onset arthritis. Scar tissue everywhere. Neural damage. You say this body came this way?"

"Well, mostly. Some of the trauma was from abuse as an infant." The little demon sounded apologetic.

Grantupoemoeunanii grimaced.

They knew there were certain rules, of course. And of course they agreed with the divine reasoning that it was better to send a demon in an infant body to expose a human who would hurt children than an actual human soul. But still. "I really do wish Hell did more to punish people like that."

"Doesn't it?" the young demon asked.

"No, not technically," Grantupoemoeunanii said, slightly distracted by trying to match the body to a demon in the system. "The humans punish themselves. Always have. All it takes for a human to get into Heaven is—huh—are you sure you were in the system? I can't find this body registered to anyone."

The young demon shrugged. "Pretty sure? Maybe?"

"Maybe?" Grantupoemoeunanii focused three flaming eyes on the little demon. "Maybe?"

Even in the human body, the demon was able to display all the hallmarks of a guilty conscience: averted eyes, tightened jaw, the smell of guilt and lies filling the air like a garden of *Lilium regale* on a summer's evening.

Work hadn't even started yet and Grantupoemoeunanii had a problem on their sticky hands.

The sentence ran through their head again with the speed of short-faced running bear: Work. Hadn't. Started. Yet.

Officially Grantupoemoeunanii was not on duty.

This didn't need to be on the books. It could be a friendly chat between two infernal and immortal co-workers. A piece of mentoring.

Grantupoemoeunanii's gummy face stretched into a beneficent smile. "In a bit of a rush when you headed out?"

"That's what the doctors said," the young demon agreed.

"Tell you what," Grantupoemoeunanii said as they vanished the computer away. "I'll give you a free tune-up, get the mortal form you're in running in tip-top condition, and you will promise not to damage it in any way until the return date. After all, fifty-two years of mortal time will be over in the blink of any eye."

The little demon blinked two creepily human eyes. "Fifty-two?"

"Did you sleep through training?" Grantupoemoeunanii asked. "You get the age of a tree in this body. Seventy-five mortal years. Sure, they say you can stretch it, but then you're borrowing time from Heaven and where does that get you?"

"Um…"

"It gets you poor retirement benefits and boredom. Better to hurry home, take your vacation days, and get started with the new job. Right?"

The little demon seemed to consider this. "Right. I guess. I just… I don't know. If I'm not in pain I might want more life."

"That's a choice," Grantupoemoeunanii admitted most grudgingly. "Not the one I'd make, personally, but if you last that long and still want to stay, that's between you and central processing." They picked the widget from their desk that reset bodies.

It wasn't much to look at, a simple faceted glass vial that caught the light, with silver and gold glitter inside. It sparkled, illuminating the room like an angel's smile.

Grantupoemoeunanii popped the crystal cork off, dapped a pinch of divine healing on their large hands, and blew it into the face of the little demon.

The tightness around their eyes faded into an expression of ecstasy. Their limbs loosened, losing their tight, hunched form. "Wow! This is amazing! I feel... I don't feel pain. None at all. My head isn't echoing with every wrong thing I've ever done. I don't hate myself!"

Grantupoemoeunanii suppressed a chuckle. "That will happen when the human form isn't broken. And, now, I need to clock in. Scurry along, little imp. There's humans to tempt and forms to file!"

"Right... Thanks!" The little demon turned proverbial tail and sprinted along the Eternal Infernal Hall.

Oh, Erowbbaia was going to be delighted with this story when they met for lunch in several hundred mortal years. Young demons were so cute. So enthusiastic.

Had Grantupoemoeunanii ever been like that? They couldn't remember. Those were the early days of the first Hells, when creatures like them were summoned forth to protect fragile human minds from wisdom beyond their comprehension.

A chime rang a celestial harmony, signaling the start of the work day.

And then there was a thump.

The whole hall shuddered.

A pack of hellhounds raced through, looking like the nightmares of Neanderthal man (which they were) as foot soldiers of hell charged through the hall.

"Grantupoemoeunanii!!!"

Their name echoed, bellowed by a voice that sounded like plagues and famine. War drums shook the ground as Bellonairnalai, Hunter of the Second Hell, approached with gnashing teeth.

"Hello, Bell," Grantupoemoeunanii said pleasantly. "Having a bit of excitement today?"

"A human has entered the hells."

"Yes, they do have a tendency to do that," Grantupoemoeunanii said. "Did this one die prematurely?"

"No, they entered fully alive. In an intact body."

Grantupoemoeunanii blinked in infernal surprise. "What? Through the bookstore in Queens? I did say that was a risk."

"The portal has been there since before humans figured out fire! We couldn't just move it," said Bellonairnalai.

"Still, it seems like an obvious sort of problem. When portals are left open, humans come traipsing in and out all the time. Stealing souls, gold, rocks. They are weird." Why *did* humans love shiny rocks so much? Grantupoemoeunanii had never understood, but there was probably a book about it somewhere. Maybe they'd take the time to read it when they finished the 299,999 books in the current series they were reading.

"Very weird." Bellonairnalai rested taloned claws on the counter. "Listen, Poemoe, I hate to do this, but the air here smells of human. Positively reeks of potential good. You didn't, maybe accidentally, let one go through here?"

Grantupoemoeunanii considered the little demon that had scampered through. "Mmmm. Nope."

"You're certain."

"Quite certain."

"Only, it's the sixth one this month that's been found near your office."

"Really?" Grantupoemoeunanii adjusted their features into a rictus of cherry-flavored horror. "That's just... Well... I don't know what to say. It's hardly like I put a poster up in the book shop advertising health, healing, or a cure for genetic diseases. That's not part of my job description."

"Mm hmm." Bellonairnalai's tusked face wrinkled into a nightmarish vision of suspicion. "You wouldn't lie to me, would you, Poemoe?"

Grantupoemoeunanii held up a jellied hand. "I am a demon of my word. No posters."

"And no Instagram."

Grantupoemoeunanii resettled in their cushy seat. "I never said that."

Bellonairnalai rolled several sets of insectoid eyes that glimmered with a malevolent hatred for all things living, but in a friendly and conspiring way. "Right. Well. I can honestly say I did my job and questioned you. I'm glad we're very clear on this. You are not— I repeat not—healing humans with some infernal magic reserved for demons."

"I most certainly am not," Grantupoemoeunanii promised.

Their friend, Hunter of the Second Hell, nodded. "Good. Then we won't say any more of it. On to other things… Are you going to the party this weekend in Nirvana? I hear there will be honey cakes."

"Erowbbaia and I were planning a trip to the Falls of the Moon's Sorrow," Grantupoemoeunanii said. "It's been ages since we went. But say hello to everyone for me."

"Sure. Anything you need while I'm on that side of eternity?"

"Oh, well, since you offered, I could use a little more divine healing. Just a bottle or three, if you have time to pick them up." They radiated hellish innocence and genuine appreciation.

It smelled faintly of apples.

Narrowing several eyes, Bellonairnalai leaned forward menacingly. Three sparkling vials rolled out from under their talons. "No. I won't have time for that."

"Well then, don't trouble yourself. Enjoy the party." They let the three vials of divine healing fall into a neglectfully open drawer that should have been locked.

Bellonairnalai whistled, calling their baying hounds to their side, and sauntered away, whistling the music of the spheres.

Grantupoemoeunanii sighed happily, breathing out the sound of iced tree limbs and sharp skates on frozen ponds.

It was just another day in hell.

THE MAKING OF *JUST ANOTHER DAY IN HELL*

I was born with an incurable genetic disease, so you can guess where this story comes from. There's a running joke in the disabled community about how a demon would react if one tried to possess our bodies. The constant pain. The brokenness. The draining fatigue. Yeah... I can't see anyone staying unless they had no other choice.

And the idea of a demon who liked humans (enough, anyway) and felt like helping amused me. So here we are, with a lovely version of Hell that isn't quite so hellish. Remember, you have friends all around. ;)

Read more by Liana Brooks!

ALL I WANT FOR CHRISTMAS IS A REAPER

THREE O'CLOCK ON A THURSDAY AFTERNOON IN APRIL, and I had an unplanned three-day weekend. In Chicago, my favorite city in the world. There were thunderheads gathering over Lake Michigan with the smell of rain in the air but, for now, downtown was a delightful playground of rushing cars, stressed commuters, and the bitter tears of lives I'd ruined with a pink slip.[1]

With nowhere in particular to be, I meandered, crossing Clark Street at the light to

---

[1] Technically this is a lie. Dulcie Waterhouse ruined her own life by embezzling from her firm and taking too many long lunch breaks buying macarons across town. The only tears were the tears of joy in her co-workers' eyes when they realized she was leaving for good. And there wasn't a pink slip. I con-vinced her to resign. I'm good like that.

reach a small city park with maple trees that wouldn't reach maturity in this century, a little playground with a sun shade, and a recycled rubber tire running track that crossed through the limited greenspace like a drunken snake trying to bite its own tail.

It was too early for school to be out and too late for lunch, which meant the park was populated by a muddy handful of toddlers, their attendant adults, and me. I kept to the outside track, crossing a stone footbridge over a shallow dirt ditch that might become a small pond if it rained. Tulips bobbed in the wind. The forsythia was out.

Little flowers and cheeky sparrows.

I enjoyed it for about four minutes before I could feel my brain scrabbling around like a trapped rat desperate for escape.

Natural vistas had that effect on me. I needed something to think about. A job to focus on. Numbers. Problems. City things.

At the sound of a jogger approaching, I stepped to the side so they could sweep past and catch the running track.

And sweep past he did. A gloriously muscular runner with olive-toned tan skin, a shock of silver-white hair shaved on the sides and long on top, a well-defined back and legs, and a black shirt sliding out of his waistband and dropping to the ground.

Well then.

It wasn't quite the young Miss Bennet dropping her gloves so a militia man could retrieve them for her, but it was possibly the twenty-first century equivalent. Even if it wasn't, it was only polite to collect the handsome man's shirt and return it to him.

I picked it up, shook off the dust and grass clippings, and held the sandalwood-scented shirt up for inspection. The owner was broad shouldered and the shirt was lean cut, meant to hug him and give everyone looking an excellent view of his well-defined muscles. Slightly more interesting was the word KILLER written across the front of the shirt in the font of the well-known horror brand, Slasher.

The jogger was a scary movie fan.

Not a lot to work with as openings went.

Scary movies weren't my cup of cocoa. No movies were, most days. Sitting still for hours on end listening to other people talk made me restless.

Perhaps it wasn't meant to be.

I folded the shirt neatly, and when I looked up the jogger was watching me from the bend of the running track only a few feet away, one white earbud hanging off his shoulder, the other still in his ear. He was younger than the white hair suggested, maybe twenties or early thirties, with dark brown—nearly black—eyes, high cheek-bones, a well-defined jaw line, and a sharp, straight nose. He looked exceptionally intense and unquantifiably captivating.

"Is that my shirt?" he asked in a deep voice as delicious as he was. I could listen to that man read the dictionary and I'd love every moment of it.

I held the shirt up, letting it unfurl over my dress. "I don't know, do you think it's mine?" I let him get a good look at me. Large, dark reds curls that looked a century out of date, a pink flower tucked behind my ear, pink lipstick, pretty smile, A-line green dress with pink flowers embroidered on it and a crinoline underneath for volume; I looked like a piece of walking history.

Twee. Sweet. Friendly.

Stupid.

I'd heard every verdict, but the dress

made me look fabulous and I loved bringing a pop of cheer to people's otherwise blighted lives.

"It'd look good on you. Killer." The corner of his mouth lifted in a sexy smile.

Oh. *No*. I did *not* like that.

Actually, I did, very much, but I knew where sexy smiles led. It would be hot nightclubs, wild parties, and then a trip to the suburbs as Mr. Sexy waxed lyrical about 'getting away from the city.' Pretty soon he'd be browsing baby name websites and talking about getting a dog.

No.

If a *Timberwolf Town*[2] werewolf couldn't tempt me, then a yappy little dog suitable for the suburbs didn't stand a chance.

I held the shirt to my shoulders and tried not to notice how good it smelled—sandalwood with an undertone of mint. The scent

---

[2] A paranormal-horror series from the mid 20s that centered around a hidden werewolf population and their unrivaled basketball team. I'm 90% certain that the ratings were due to the regular shower scenes.

was too light for a cologne—probably a soap. "It looks like my size, too." Assuming it was supposed to be worn halfway to my knees. Jogging, dark, and handsome was also tall, dark, and handsome.

"I'll let you borrow it some time." The man had dark, hungry eyes that promised to make my flirtation worth my time.

"Sure." That was never going to happen. I tossed the shirt to him. "Enjoy your run."

The smile turned to a smirk. "Enjoy the view." He secured the shirt to his waistband again and took off with a wink.

Confidence was always sexy, and I was very tempted to continue my little stroll around the park and see if the jogger wanted to join me for a post-workout snack somewhere.

I was great at first dates. Lots of confidence and a big smile got me everything I wanted.

Second dates?

No one had tempted me enough to schedule a second date since college.

I glanced at the jogger again. *Maybe* no one had tempted me?

He looked familiar in that we–met–once–

in–passing sort of way.

My memory for names and faces was legendary, but I couldn't recall being introduced to him before.

It was going to bother me all afternoon if I didn't pursue it.

As if the office had a psychic link,[3] my phone rang, the quick staccato tattoo reserved for my boss. Work was there again, to rescue me from my worst impulses and save me from the kind of heartbreak ice cream couldn't fix.

"Hi, Amara." I moved toward the crosswalk, dodging a little green car that nearly swerved into me.

Chicago drivers. So charming.

There was a tiny community garden space across the street, a safe distance from the sexy jogger.

"Merri, I just heard the good word from Windy City Security, you've officially slayed the wicked witch of the upper west side. Did you break seven minutes?" Amara Rosa

---

[3] Or, let's be honest, a stopwatch to keep track of the betting on the Dulcie Waterhouse situation.

Park[4] was just as competitive as I was and she'd had my back in the office betting pool.

Sloan and Markham is *the* name in corporate accounting in Illinois. Amara is the head of the forensic accounting unit.

Really, we're a bunch of math nerds who read too many mystery novels and decided we'd grow up to fight white collar crime for a six-figure annual salary. And in the land of the nerds, I'm the big, brutal boss, the final, unconquerable hurdle.

"Six minutes," I said with a killer smile.[5]

"You make me so happy! Did Dulcie cry? I met her when I went in for the initial contact and…" Amara sighed. "Some people just *look* evil, you know?"

I pictured Dulcie Waterhouse in her gray pantsuit with a black silk shell under the jacket, two silver studs in each ear, a professional, asymmetrical cut for her dark brown hair, and dark red lipstick on a mouth pouring out more cuss words than could fit into a Monday morning commute when the

---

[4] Named for Amara Enyia and Rosa Parks, obviously.

[5] Ha ha, I'm so funny!

trains were down. "She didn't cry, but you may need to give the interns a bonus for reading my emails for the next few weeks."

"More death threats?" Amara sighed again. "What is it about you that attracts so much venom?"

"It's the job." And the fact that dressing like the lead singer from a retro throwback band made everyone underestimate me. What can I say? I have brains *and* beauty.

With a click of her tongue, Amara dismissed the disappointing news. "Well, done is done. I'll give the interns a heads up." There was a chime in the background. "Oh, and there's the first hit on social media. Want to hear it?"

"It's not like I'm going to look it up." I didn't do social media. Despite having an email assigned to me along with my social security number, I had the digital footprint of a ghost.

"The headline is 'Chicago's Infamous Grim Reaper Strikes Again.' Good job."

"I try my best."

Amara made a happy, purring sound. "Did you try your very best with Harry?"

"Harry?" I stopped in front of a bench.

"I'm drawing a blank."

"Junior executive in accounting?" Amara dangled the tidbit.

Mentally I flipped through a detailed list of junior accounting people. "Not ringing any bells."

"Henderson account?"

I shuddered.

"He sent you a gorgeous bouquet of day lilies—"

"He was telling me about how his parents were building a new house in Sugar Grove and how the commute was under thirty minutes to the city with the new high-speed trains."

There was a stunned silence and then Amara took a deep breath. "So…"

"So, thanks but no thanks? Give them to someone else."

"He left a note too."

Stupid man. But it was only polite to read the note and find some excuse for why I couldn't show up to Domestication Of The Wild Wifey 101. "Leave it on my desk. I'll deal with it when I get back to the office."

"About that…."

"You have another job for me before the weekend?" If there were gods who smiled fondly on math nerds, I would have prayed. Numbers and patterns were my favorite candy. A weekend sorting through someone else's finances as just as blissful as a bubble bath.

There was a hesitant little sigh, which meant Amara wasn't sold on the job but someone was begging. "This is an odd one. It's not the bosses calling, it's an employee, and she asked for you by name because she said you worked here, but she didn't seem to know what it is you do."

Weird. "The name?"

"Ellen Berry."

Someone else would have a hazy memory of a schoolyard friend who they'd met during a game of tag–turned–head–on–collision in kindergarten.

My memory was sharper than that, and off the top of my head I could rattle off all the major life events in Ellen's personal history up until she left for college in New York. We hadn't kept in touch mostly because I forgot people existed when I was working with math.

It was great for my bank account, but not for relationships.

"Merri?" Amara waited. "If I give you the address can you go over and see what's going on?"

"Sure. Where am I headed?"

"Cozy Studios—"

"Cozy as in Cozy TV with the candy-dipped romances?" Good grief. "Can I fire the writers for their poor plotlines?"

"Only if they're embezzling," Amara said. "Otherwise, give them the quick two-day special. A little workflow advice. A little hiring advice. And then get out of there, because we have the Oretega account to tackle next week."

Easy as mud pie in Mississippi. "Got it. In. Out. Tear-free."

"If you make it tear-free, I will personally buy you dinner anywhere in the city."

"I like expensive food," I warned.

"Cozy was just bought out by Slasher Corp," Amara reported with maybe just a soupçon of glee. "You're getting called in because Cozy is getting killed."

Keep reading! Head to
<u>www.inkprintpress.com/
lianabrooks/christmas/reaper/</u>
to buy your copy now!

ABOUT THE AUTHOR

LIANA BROOKS would love to sign up for the android revolution if it guaranteed her a new body. Until then, Liana distracts herself writing science fiction in every form, from sprawling space operas romances (the *Fleet of Malik* series) to the antics of a super-powered family (the *Heroes and Villains* series).

Liana also maintains a soft spot for paranormal romances. She writes the popular *All I Want For Christmas* novellas, including *All I Want For Christmas Is A Werewolf* and *All I Want For Christmas Is A Reaper*.

You can learn more about her and her books at www.LianaBrooks.com.

INKLETS

Collect them all! Released on the 1st and 15th of each month.

Shadows NEVER LIE
AMY LAURENS

Here She Lies
LIANA BROOKS

Perfect Destruction
An Age Of Unicorns Story
AMY LAURENS

What Blood Can Do
AMY LAURENS

Dancer, Dreamer Seer
LIANA BROOKS

As Time Whirls Slowly Past
AMY LAURENS

Far More Satisfying Than Hell
AMY LAURENS

Just Another Day In Hell
LIANA BROOKS

Moon AND Morning
AMY LAURENS

Some
Impropriety
Expected
AMY LAURENS

NEON SNOW
LIANA BROOKS

Reincarnation
LIANA BROOKS

More Than
Mushrooms
AMY LAURENS

DOUBLE ISSUE
How To Make A Star
& The World Ended
LIANA BROOKS

CAUGHT
IN THE ACT
AMY LAURENS

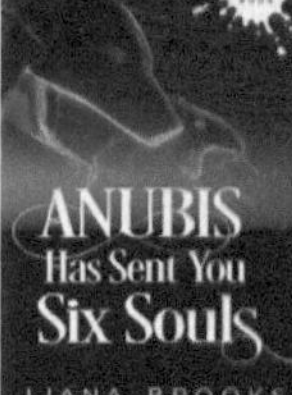

ANUBIS
Has Sent You
Six Souls
LIANA BROOKS

PRAYER TO A
GODDESS
LIANA BROOKS

Love In The
Time Of Corona
AMY LAURENS